I read this book all by myself

....

For everyone at Antwerp International School – JC
For Dizzie and Enid – AP

A Red Fox Book

Published by Random House Children's Books
61-63 Uxbridge Road, London W5 5SA

A division of the Random House Group Ltd
London Melbourne Sydney Auckland
Johannesburg and agencies throughout the world

3 5 7 9 10 8 6 4 2

First published in Great Britain by Red Fox 2001

Published in hardback by Heinemann Library, a division of
Reed Educational and Professional Publishing Limited,
by arrangement with Random House Children's Books

Printed in Singapore by Tien Wah Press

THE RANDOM HOUSE GROUP Limited Reg. No. 954009
www.kidsatrandomhouse.co.uk

ISBN 0 09 941743 X (paperback)
ISBN 0 431 02408 1 (hardback)

Sherman Swaps Shells

Jane Clarke
Ant Parker

RED FOX

To George

Happy Third Birthday!

Very best wishes

from

Jane Clarke

1 May 2006

"Sherman," said Mum, "you need a new shell."

"But I like this one," Sherman said.

"Look at the state of it! You've chipped it playing clawball. It won't keep you safe any more."

"I'll be careful," Sherman said.

your old shell is worn out.

But I like it like this!

"It's covered in tar and it's much too small," Mum said. "Your shell doesn't fit you any more. You've grown out of it."

"There's plenty of room at the end!" Sherman wriggled his tail. It scraped against the pebble collection he kept at the bottom of his shell.

I hate swapping.

Let's go swapping.

"You can't wear the same shell forever,"
said Mum. "It's time for you to swap shells."
Mum took Sherman by the claw. They
scuttled to the shell heap.

7

"There's lots to choose from," said Mum. "The waves bring in new shells all the time. This looks like a good one. Try it on."

"Someone might see," Sherman said.

"There's no need to be shy," Mum said.

Sherman tried it on. "It's too tight," he said.

"Yes," said Mum. "How about that green one over there?"

Sherman slipped out of his old shell and into the green one.

"It's very smart," said Mum.

"It's very heavy," said Sherman.

"It's just right," said Mum.

Oh, Sherman, you do look nice!

I want one like that!

A teenager strolled past. He was wearing a shell with huge spikes.

"Wow!" said Sherman. "Can I have one of those? Please?"

"Those shells are hard to find in your size," Mum said.

"Here's one," said Sherman. "I'll try it on."
"It's far too big," said Mum.

It doesn't fit.

"Everyone's wearing them like this,"
said Sherman.

"Take it off," said Mum. "You can have
one when you're older."

"It's not fair," said Sherman.

"How about this one?" Mum said.
"It's just like your old shell. Put it on."
   "Do I have to?"
   "Yes," said Mum. "If you're good,
I'll take you to Urchin Express."
   Sherman dived out of his old shell into
the new one.

"Get out of my shell!" roared a voice.

Sherman shot out backwards.

"Didn't your mother teach you to knock?" the old hermit crab grumbled.

"Sherman!" Mum was lobster pink.

"I'm very sorry," she told the old crab. "He needs a new shell, you see. Come along, Sherman. We'll look over there."

Sherman scuttled to the top of the shell heap.

I'm stuck!

"I like this one," he said,
pointing to a spiky shell.

"It will never fit," Mum said.

"It will, look." Sherman squeezed into
the shell. "It's a bit tight," he said.

"Take it off then," said Mum.

"Mum!" Sherman tried to wriggle out of the shell. "I'm stuck . . ."

"I knew it," said Mum. "Our bodies curve to the right. Most shells have spirals that curve to the right. This one curves to the left. That's why you're stuck."

"I'll pull you out," Mum said.
She grabbed Sherman's legs with her
powerful claws and heaved.

"Ooooooof!"

Sherman popped out. He counted his
legs. They were all still there. He slunk
back into his old shell.

"Now Sherman," Mum said. "We can spend all day trying to find another shell. Or we can go back and get the green one that was just right, and go to Urchin Express."

"What's the tide?" asked Sherman.

"High tide. There will be plenty of fresh plankton."

"Okay," said Sherman, "we'll get the green shell."

Sherman swapped shells. He emptied his pebble collection into the bottom of the new shell. There was plenty of room inside.

He could collect more now.

"What shall I do with my old shell?"
asked Sherman.

"Leave it here," said Mum. "Someone
else might want it."

Sherman patted the shell with
his claw. "Goodbye, Old Shell,"
he said. "I'll miss you."

It was fun playing clawball with you.

25

Urchin Express was very busy. It was full of young anemones waving their tentacles. There was a long queue. They crawled towards the counter.

Why are those limpets pushing?

They ordered, and
found an empty rock
and sat down.

"How's the plankton
shake?" asked Mum.
"Delicious." Sherman
slurped the last drops
through the straw.

"Disgusting," said Mum.
"It isn't even dead yet."
She nibbled on
her piece of
rotten fish.

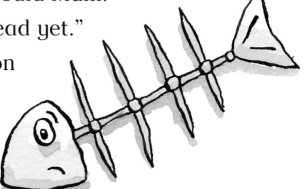

"My new shell is heavy," Sherman said.

"It's a good solid shell," said Mum. "Very sensible."

"It would look great with anemones stuck on it," said Sherman.

"You're not sticking anemones on a brand new shell!" said Mum.

"But anemones are cool!" said Sherman. "And they're great for playing tide-and-seek. No one would find me if I had anemones on my shell. Why can't I have anemones? It's not fair! I wish I had my old shell back!"

"Cheer up!" Mum said. "Worse things happen at sea."

Anemones are silly!

Suddenly a shadow blotted out the sun. Urchin Express went dark. The shadow reached into the rock pool.

I'm off!

Hide!

33

The shadow scooped up Sherman!
Higher and higher he went. Higher than
high tide.

Sherman was frightened. He hid inside his
new shell. The shadow's giant claw turned
him upside down.

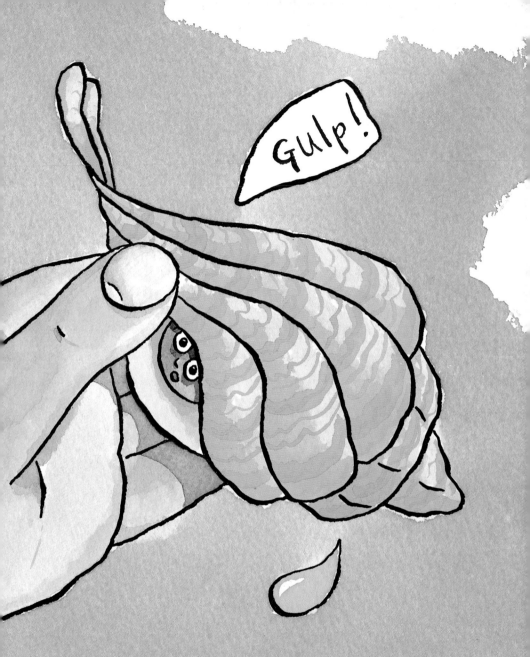

"This is a nice shell," the shadow said.

"I think I'll keep it."

It nipped me!

"I'm not a shell! I'm a hermit crab!"
Sherman nipped the shadow as hard as he
could. The shadow yelled,

"Ow, ow, ow!"

36

Sherman **flew** through the air.

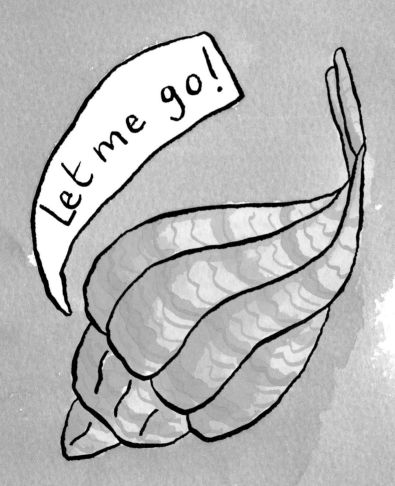

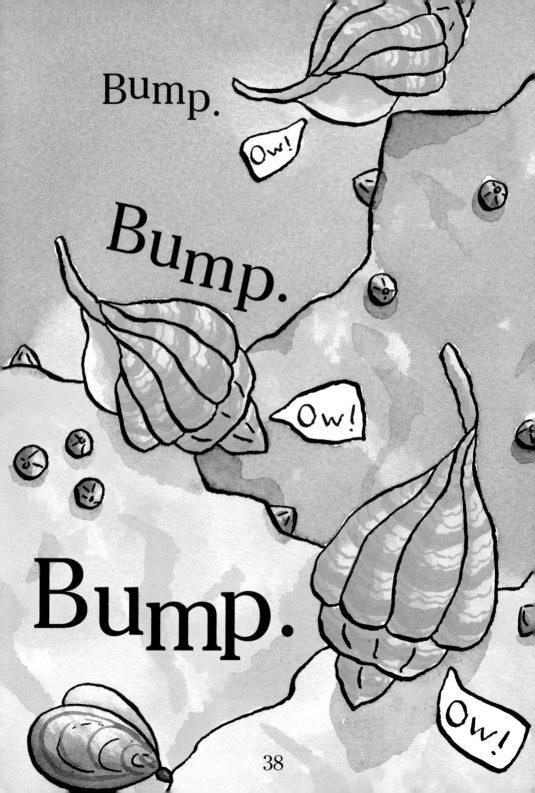

Sherman bounced down the rocks and fell into the pool.

Sunlight danced across the rock pool. The shadow was gone.

Plop.

"Sherman! Are you okay?"

"I . . . I think so."

"It's a good job you were wearing your new shell," said Mum. "Your old one would have broken!"

40

"What was that shadow?" Sherman asked.

"It was a Person," Mum said. "You have to hide from People."

"People wouldn't see me if I had anemones on my shell."

"Hmmm," said Mum.

I might get some too!

"So can I stick anemones on my shell?"

"Okay," said Mum.

"Great!" said Sherman. "I think I'll like my new shell."

Get your anemones here.

No one will find me now!

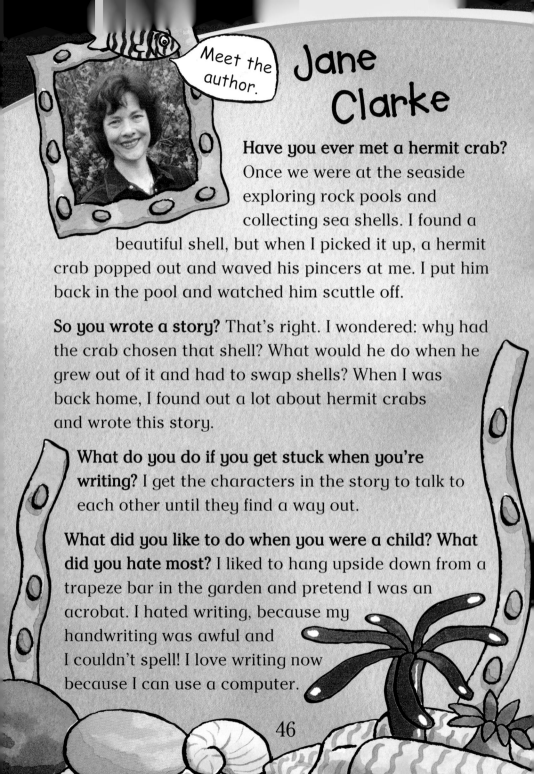

Jane Clarke

Have you ever met a hermit crab? Once we were at the seaside exploring rock pools and collecting sea shells. I found a beautiful shell, but when I picked it up, a hermit crab popped out and waved his pincers at me. I put him back in the pool and watched him scuttle off.

So you wrote a story? That's right. I wondered: why had the crab chosen that shell? What would he do when he grew out of it and had to swap shells? When I was back home, I found out a lot about hermit crabs and wrote this story.

What do you do if you get stuck when you're writing? I get the characters in the story to talk to each other until they find a way out.

What did you like to do when you were a child? What did you hate most? I liked to hang upside down from a trapeze bar in the garden and pretend I was an acrobat. I hated writing, because my handwriting was awful and I couldn't spell! I love writing now because I can use a computer.

46

Ant Parker

Meet the illustrator.

Have you ever met a hermit crab? I grew up a long way from the sea, but we went on school field trips to visit the coast. We would collect things and bring them back – not living things of course! I don't think I ever saw a hermit crab, but we found shrimps, starfish and jellyfish.

How long did it take to paint the pictures in this book? Shells are quite difficult to draw so I had to do a lot of research. I found some very good sites about hermit crabs on the internet. Then I drew the pictures in pencil. Next, I painted them with ink and watercolour. This last bit took about a month.

Where do you live? I live in London, but I go to the coast a lot. In summer, I go swimming. In winter, I go on long walks with my dog Bramble. She likes to roll in the seaweed left by high tide. Often she comes home with old crab shells stuck in her coat!

Did you always like to draw? I have liked to draw since I was very young.

Will you try and write or draw a story?

Let your ideas take flight with
Flying Foxes

All the Little Ones – and a Half
by Mary Murphy

Sherman Swaps Shells
by Jane Clarke and Ant Parker

Digging for Dinosaurs
by Judy Waite and Garry Parsons

Shadowhog
by Sandra Ann Horn and Mary McQuillan

The Magic Backpack
by Julia Jarman and Adriano Gon

Jake and the Red Bird
by Ragnhild Scamell and Valeria Petrone

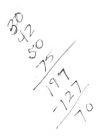